THREE LOONS

by

Mark Schlitt

Copyright © 2007

ISBN: 9798681825234

Contents

the kids at the local theater. Meanwhile the guys practically inhaled their food with only a few quips and jokes about girls and shopping in order to move on to the important task at hand.

As soon as their plates were in the sink, it was a dash for the garage where the men outfitted Jay's 21' Thunder Jet fishing boat with their newest gear and more bait than they could ever need "just to be safe".

When they handed each rod, tackle box, extra spool of line and accessory up to Jay, who stood in the boat, they extolled its virtues as if it was their own creation or their newest child. They delivered facts, figures, and statistics, discussed breaking strength, stretch, abrasion resistance, the advantages of nylon over silk, hook sizes, treble vs circle as if they were the world's experts. Jay took each item, smiled his dubious smile, or belched his amused chuckle, shook his head, and found its perfect place in hatches, or compartments from aft to bow. Jay had a gift for quickly organizing every little detail ensuring safety as well as easy accessibility.

It would be only their third fishing trip of the year, and so close to winter, it was sure to be the last. The guys unanimously agreed they needed to go fishing more often and promised to "make it happen" next year.

* *

The tradition after each successful trip was to invite friends, relatives, bosses, co-workers, and neighbors to enjoy the feasting and storytelling. Nearly as much fun as the fishing was frying, poaching, grilling and sharing the bounty. All three guys greatly enjoyed experimenting with their newest recipes, spice combinations and exotic sauces, to the accolades and star ratings or rebuke and gagging imitations of the partying, partially sober horde. All the while slightly embellished fish stories, corroborated, exaggerated or disputed by the participants were playfully and passionately recounted to impress and amuse the crowd and relive the adventure.

* *

CHAPTER THREE

Daddy's Girl

Jay was engrossed with every detail of the upcoming adventure as he poured freshly brewed coffee into his cup, then carefully poured the remaining coffee into a thermos for the drive to the boat ramp. He moved quickly but quietly to keep from disturbing his sleeping beauties just down the hall.

* * * * * * * * * * * * * * * * * * * *

As much as Jay loved Shanna, Jaece was his treasure, his joy, the one he spoiled and would do anything for. She was their only child and a definite "daddy's girl" who was normally waiting at the front door when he came home exhausted from work. Whether with beaming face and outstretched arms, or one of her cute antics, she could make Jay laugh and his stress melt away, no matter how difficult the day had been. Sometimes he would sit for hours telling his precious little princess, crazy, outlandish stories using constantly changing voice inflections, sometimes whispers, followed by loud boisterous tones and wild gestures. Jay's imagination and verbal prowess amused and amazed everyone. Jaece would watch his every expression and movement, listening in total captivation, hanging on every word. Sometimes she would giggle then crouch covering her face and the next moment burst out laughing, her little body quaking. Who enjoyed those times

9

more was impossible to know, but there was no

doubt the love and adoration they shared was unique

and very special.

* * * * * * * * * * * * * * * * * * * *

CHAPTER FOUR

Marvelous Day

Jay heard the truck pull up out front as he was carrying the last cooler filled with beer and sandwiches to the boat. Daniel's Dodge Ram, diesel crew cab pickup was not only his "pride and joy" it was also the most practical vehicle for the thirty minute ride to the boat ramp.

Daniel was the most athletic and muscular of the three, having an amazingly low six-percent body fat. He owned his own truck repair business and could outwork any employee he had ever hired. Much to his wife's chagrin all Susan's female friends referred to Daniel as her "buff spouse" always reminding her how lucky she was.

Daniel backed the truck toward the trailer's tongue until Jay gave him the signal to stop. Jay jumped down from the boat as James jumped out of the truck, ran to the back, and in thirty seconds the boat was secured, lights plugged in and they were on their way.

The three joked all the way to the dock, becoming louder and more animated as their excitement grew. Bets were placed on who would catch the first fish, who would catch the biggest, and who would catch the most. It was sure to be a fun-filled enjoyable day, but bragging rights would make the following day even more memorable for one of them.

The sky was turning crimson toward the east as Jay maneuvered the boat through the no-wake zones. He took this opportunity while it was relatively quiet and calm to let everyone know where he had secured each piece of their gear. It was immediately obvious to the others how orderly and tidy the boat had been packed making it easy to move around if and hopefully when things got hectic trying to catch and secure their haul. The lecture ended in twenty minutes, just as they were able to go full throttle toward the spot they had marked on the GPS their last time out.

The ocean was relatively calm with two-foot chop off shore. Jay's Thunder Jet with its big Evinrude E-TEC 135 HP motor cut right through the small waves and in less than ninety minutes they would set anchor. The rods and reels were already "locked and loaded" and ready to go, so all they had to do was cut squid and herring to hide their hooks and tempt the fish living 250 feet below.

It was a marvelous day! The weather forecast was for calm seas and partly cloudy skies until a major, fast moving front was forecast to blast through late that night or early the next morning bringing heavy rain, sleet and high winds. With a little luck, they would be limited out and on the way home before the seas became uncomfortably rough.

* *

<u>CHAPTER FIVE</u>

Looney Entertainment

Jay couldn't resist heading straight toward a small group of loons floating in the water in the boat's path. The small black birds with white bands on their wings were plentiful today floating on the water in groups of three to six, totally oblivious to the noisy boat.

It was always a hoot to see how the loons would react when Jay aimed straight toward the little black spots. When the boat was only ten yards away, one flapped its wings and appeared to be running on the water for a hundred feet before it finally became airborne and flew away from the aggravation while the other two dived into the dark water. All three in the boat laughed at the entertaining sight. When the boat was twenty yards beyond where the three birds had been minding their own business, the two submerged loons popped out of the water and resumed their activities while the third slowly circled back and plopped down with its friends.

* * * * * * * * * * * * * * * * * * * *

CHAPTER SIX

Anchor Away

It was no longer dark when Jay slowed the boat to locate the exact spot marked on his GPS. Daniel and James high fived and began readying the rods and cutting bait. Jay killed the motor, moved to the bow of the boat, climbed out, and opened the hatch that housed the anchor. He looked around for a landmark, then realized that even with unlimited visibility they were surrounded by water as far as the eye could see. It was no problem because, with the GPS, they really didn't need landmarks.

Jay stood with toes out over the bow's edge, held the anchor away from the side, and dropped it into the water. Someday he would rig a motor for the tough job of pulling the heavy anchor back up from the bottom and into the boat, but for now he had two willing helpers to do the hard part. Normally it only took a bit of chiding to get one of them to take up the task. "I'll bet five dollars you can't get the anchor in the boat in ten minutes...starting ten, nine..." By the time he got to five someone always ran toward the front of the boat hoping to do the impossible.

The first 50 feet attached to the anchor was chain, followed by another 300 feet of ski rope. Jay held the chain and rope out away from the edge so they wouldn't scuff his beautiful baby. He also required anyone who pulled the anchor up to do the same. It was easy to understand why Jay quickly

jumped to the front after he reached the right spot.

It sometimes took twenty minutes of sweating,

grunting and flexing, with muscles burning to haul

the anchor back into the boat, whereas five minutes

and almost no effort found the anchor on the ocean

floor.

"Hey Jay! Don't fall in." chided James.

"See if you can hang your feet further over

the edge." added Daniel.

Then both jumped toward port simultaneously

rocking the boat. For a split second, Jay did the

dizzy dance trying to maintain his balance but

landed on his rear barely avoiding going overboard.

"You jerks!" he yelled, furious. But looking

back at the two falling over laughing only started

him laughing aloud, remembering some of the tricks he had pulled on them in the past.

Jay tied off the rope and watched the GPS as the current turned the boat. Within minutes, it was obvious the anchor had found a solid resting place since they were no longer drifting.

Jay made his way to the back of the boat and proudly announced that "the captain" was ready for a beer. The cooler lid opened, three beers were produced and with the traditional clinking of the bottles the fishing began.

* *

<u>CHAPTER SEVEN</u>

The Fight Begins

Fishing for halibut 250 feet deep can be incredibly boring, if the fish are not in the area or aren't hungry. But it can also be a real firestorm of activity if three poles are getting bites at once. Though everybody hoped to catch the biggest, the most, and the first, they knew, even if the fishing was slow, they were going to have a great time.

The beer was flowing, the snacks and sandwiches were delicious, and the jokes and hyperbole filled stories were entertaining. Discussing the challenges at work, bragging about accomplishments, talking about the win of their favorite sports team, laughing about the funniest thing one of the kids did or said, filled the time while waiting for the fish to find the tasty morsels floating a few feet off the ocean bottom.

Suddenly Daniel jumped up, spilling his beer as his fishing rod tip dipped down, then up. He grabbed the rod from its holder, gave it a swift upward pull to set the hook and held his breath, waiting, slowly turning the reel hoping to feel a tug on the line.

James' eyes darted from his own pole to Daniel's. James was the oldest of the three and had been a prison guard for ten years until dealing with some of the dregs of society on a daily basis caused mental and physical burnout. Shortly after his tenth anniversary at the prison, he turned in his letter of resignation, and fulfilled a lifelong dream when he started his own business. James was amazingly fit for his age and competed equally well with the other two brothers-in-law no matter what the endeavor. He watched the action on Daniel's rod and hoped he would be as lucky but also didn't want to miss the opportunity if a fish nibbled his bait.

Jay was now standing in a half crouch, waiting to see which direction he would need to go. If his own line dipped, he would grab it, but if Daniel had a big one hooked, he would clear the deck moving bottles and food out of the way and readying the net or the gaff.

Daniel slowly reeled the line a few more feet when he abruptly felt the tug he had hoped for. His pole bent toward the water and the fight was on! Daniel's face lit up with a huge smile, as he realized he had a good sized one on the line. With intense concentration he struggled as he pulled the bent rod up, then reeled it down. He repeated the action again and again for several minutes as sweat poured from his forehead onto his very red but excited face.

Then came the sound all fishermen craved. The reel squealed as the line pulled away against the drag. Daniel now knew this fish was big and a fighter! It was a battle to be won or lost by his quick decisions and decisive action. James cheered when he heard the sound while Jay quickly cleared the deck, picked up and secured the fallen beer bottle and poured water onto the deck to wash away the spilled beer. A clean deck was a safe deck, he always said, and Jay knew that right now was the most important time to live that motto. To fall on a slippery deck with a gaff in hand could result in a dangerous flesh wound or even put an eye out.

25

* *

CHAPTER EIGHT

Gaff

"It's definitely a halley", Daniel yelled in a strained voice "and it feels like a big one by the way it's working the line". At this point, while the fish was fighting to swim away and get loose, all Daniel could do was hang on tight and keep the slack out of the line. This was the excitement every fisherman lived for.

"All right, way to go!" hollered James.

"Well, we've got some good eating if you don't lose him" chided Jay. The two were happy to know they had found the halibut and they were biting, yet jealous, wishing this first one, and big one, would have been theirs.

For the next twenty minutes Daniel fought the fish, pulling the rod up then reeling it down until the desperate creature would pull the line out against the drag and Daniel would once again lose much of what he had gained. This was the battle! Dragging up two hundred and fifty feet of line with a huge fish fighting to stay alive, to get away, to throw the hook, was hard work but the adrenaline and the excitement kept his mind off his tired muscles.

Jay startled James, who was concentrating on Daniel's struggle, when he shouted and pointed, "Your pole!" and James was over to his side of the boat, grabbing the pole in an instant. Now things were exciting! James tightly clutched the rod while very slowly turning the crank on the reel waiting anxiously for any action.

Was it on the line? Was it hooked well or was it just playing with the bait? His pole dipped and James yanked to set the hook. His pole bent nearly in half and the struggle began again on the other side of the boat.

Jay realized he was done fishing for the moment. His job now was to coordinate the two struggling, fighting, excited fishermen, helping whichever one needed help the most and keeping the boat free of anything that would interfere. Jay moved from side to side watching, listening, instinctively lending a hand where needed, usually before they even asked. The sound of the straining rods and the whizzing line was almost as exciting as having one on his own line, but not quite.

"Oh man! Look at this baby!" Daniel implored when he saw the grayish-black shadow of what was at least a fifty pound halibut only ten feet below the water's surface. He had been working his fish for twenty minutes and it was beginning to tire.

When Jay stuck his head over the side near Daniel, he caught a glimpse of the fish briefly before it headed south for what seemed like the tenth time. All Daniel could do was hang on to his pole with both hands and wait until the line stopped buzzing off the reel.

Jay resembled a parrot pacing in its cage, as he moved from one side of the boat to the other, head bobbing up and down watching what was happening, always ready to help out where he could. He would bark an occasional order, which was sometimes acknowledged but more often ignored.

Daniel shouted and Jay bent over the side with gaff in hand and waited for a good opportunity to hook Daniel's "big one". Daniel moved the line so the big halibut was close to Jay's gaff and in a flash Jay had it hooked. Both men groaned, as they struggled, and pulled the angry fifty or sixty pounder into the boat.

As soon as it was over the side, Jay dropped the gaff, grabbed the club, and hit the fish hard in the head. Daniel twisted his hook out of the big halibut's mouth, then cut its gills to bleed it. Meanwhile Jay freed the gaff, put it back in its place and poured numerous buckets of water all over his blood strewn deck to clean up the mess. A short while later the fish was in the ice bin where it was out of the way and kept fresh for the trip home.

* *

CHAPTER NINE

The Weigh In

Daniel put new bait on his hooks, then went to see how James was doing with his fish. Jay went back to his line and began reeling it up to check his bait.

"Damn" said Jay under his breath several minutes later when his hooks emerged. The bait was gone, picked clean while he was helping the others. Jay fixed the hooks with his special herring and squid combo then turned to see how James was faring just in time to grab the gaff and stab another big halibut.

Daniel decided that James' fish was bigger than his, but not by much as all three pulled it over the side and into the boat. Then they finished getting James' whopper bled and ready for the ice bin.

Before doing anything else, both fish had to be weighed to see whose was biggest. Daniel's came in at an impressive 55 pounds but James' topped it by six pounds, eliciting a boisterous victory yell from James and a snide, "just wait for mine" from Jay.

Both "bad boys" posed, displaying their best tough guy look while holding up their prized catches. The photos would provide proof, to back up their stories, long after the fish had been enjoyed at the dinner table.

With that important work out of the way, the fish were put back on ice. Then came the race to get the newly baited hooks back into the deep, dark, depths to the hungry fish below.

It was again time to sit and wait, which meant grabbing another sandwich and beer. The three breathlessly rattled on about the size and fight of each fish giving a moment by moment description of their action.

Jay was slightly disappointed. The first fish was Daniel's and nothing could change that. However, he still had a chance at the biggest and the most. His disappointment was short lived when he noticed his pole tip bounce down and back up.

* * * * * * * * * * * * * * * * * * * *

<u>CHAPTER TEN</u>

The Surprise

Jay was up and out of his seat in a flash. He grabbed the fishing rod with one hand, fumbled the sandwich with his other until Daniel jumped beside him and took the sandwich.

Jay carefully got set, slowly reeled the line up a few feet, and impatiently waited for a tug from below. The seconds felt like weeks as he stood motionless and waited.

Jay was oblivious to the stares of his audience, and to the waves and the bobbing of the boat. His total concentration was fixed on the feel of the pole. He sensed what was happening 250 feet below where his hooks and weight were drifting a few feet off the ocean bottom.

When nothing happened, Jay slowly reeled up his line. As he reeled, he could tell something was wrong. It felt far too heavy to be only hooks, line, and bait. Yet, whatever was on the line put up no fight at all. Several minutes later as he reeled in the last of the line, Jay understood why. Stuck on his hook was one of eight, four foot long tentacles. The other seven clung to the line along with the cephalopod's sack like body.

James and Daniel moved tenuously to the stern, and leaned over to get a better look, but kept a respectful distance. "Wow! I've never seen one up close." James admitted.

Jay carefully pulled his rod into the boat and gently let the fair sized octopus down onto the deck while freeing its barely hooked tentacle.

"I've seen them on TV and in aquariums." said Daniel moving away from the unusual creature. "Are they dangerous?" he asked, pulling out his knife, as the thing began slithering toward him.

"It sure moves fast!" Jay exclaimed, as the tentacles began reaching in all directions dragging the sack from side to side while the odd looking creature continued exploring the boat.

James reached down and touched one tentacle. The arm instantly wrapped around his finger, then his hand eliciting a laugh. "It doesn't hurt at all," he said surprised. "It's just a bunch of suction cups!"

With that, all three took turns feeling the roaming arms wrap themselves around their fingers and hands with hundreds of suction like pads. For several minutes they continued touching and picking up their new, odd looking plaything. After sufficiently satisfying their curiosity, Jay gently dropped the octopus back into the water.

They were amazed as they discussed the frightening looking creature that seemed almost playful and harmless. They each tried to describe the feeling of the suction pads on the tentacles and their surprise that it didn't hurt. They were also surprised that "Octo", as they now were calling it, seemed curious and not frightened and how gingerly the octopus moved around in the boat.

* *

CHAPTER ELEVEN

Major Changes

For the third time, Jay carefully but hurriedly, baited his hooks and lowered them toward what he hoped would be the biggest fish in the area. Then he watchfully sat down and again gobbled his sandwich and sipped his beer, while eyes darted from pole to pole.

The afternoon continued even busier than the morning. It was constant activity, punctuated by the occasional annoying dogfish or skate that had to be tossed back or cut loose. The time flew by as the ice bin filled with fish. Several halibut that would have been definite keepers on a slower day were deemed too small and were returned to their home to "grow awhile longer".

The adrenaline rush of the continuous activity made the men oblivious to the rapidly changing weather. Previously clear blue skies were quickly replaced with gray menacing clouds. Light winds became blustery, and placid water changed to four foot swells. But with the "halley" biting, the activity was non-stop. The excitement and action kept them occupied, concentrating on the fish, the poles, hooks, and bait. Keeping the cooler organized, the gaff handy and secure, and the deck clean between each catch was all encompassing and consuming, to the exclusion of everything else.

When Jay was nearly tossed from the boat as he reached over the side with the gaff, he looked up and around, surprised to see the change. "We better start getting the gear up!" he practically

shouted in alarm. Then he made the fatal mistake of

gaffing Daniel's halibut. Now they were committed

to bringing it in the boat and getting it bled and into

the ice bin. At that moment, James got another

"good one" on his line which started the nearly half-

hour process once again.

* *

CHAPTER TWELVE

Tough Decision

The thirty-degree temperature drop wasn't as worrisome as the ice cold rain that began pelting them. During the short time, the three were fighting with the fish in the boat and the one on the line the sky changed ominously from gray to black. The formerly intermittent rain, became a constant torrent.   Visibility had become so poor that while Daniel was putting his rod and rod holder away on the port side of the boat he could barely see James, still reeling his fish in on the starboard side only a few feet away.

While Jay was in the back of the boat securing his rod, he yelled at Daniel to "get the anchor up quick". The cold rain was now beating down so hard it stung. "Jay! Could you grab my rain slicker?" yelled James in pain, as he too began to grasp the gravity of the situation.

The boat was bobbing so violently now that the three had to continually hang on to something to stay on their feet. Daniel was at the bow, just starting the normally twenty plus minute task of pulling up the anchor. Jay tossed him a poncho and life preserver and moved to the back to help James.

Jay put on his own raincoat and life jacket, then grabbed James' rod so he could do the same. Drenched and shivering almost uncontrollably, Jay pulled the rod into the boat, hesitated briefly, then made one of the toughest decisions of his life as he cut the line.

That one simple deed put fear into James. Jay would never, under any circumstances he could think of, cut the line with such a good sized halibut on it. The situation must be serious. Since he no longer had a rod to worry about James slowly, arduously moved toward the bow to see if he could help Daniel with the anchor.

Daniel was lying on his stomach hanging over the bow trying to pull up the anchor without being tossed overboard. Bouncing up and down, with much of his weight over the edge on the slippery wet bow, was a difficult and dangerous task. James grabbed Daniel's legs and tried to steady him, hoping it would help speed up the progress. He realized they needed to start heading toward shore immediately if they were going to get out of this

mess alive. The three had been in some dangerous

situations before but their toughness and smart,

instinctive decisions had allowed them to prevail and

survive. This had become, in just a short time, as

bad as any he could remember.

* *

CHAPTER THIRTEEN

Frozen With Fear

Jay put James' rod away, then sat down at the controls, and started the boat's motor. He left it in neutral to warm the engine then crawled through the bulkhead into the bow's storage area and felt around like a blind man as he tried to find the flares and flare gun. There was nearly a foot of water in the boat already, so after Jay found the flares he went back to the controls and started the bilge pump.

While making his way to the bow, to see how the other two were doing with the anchor, Jay felt like a drunken sailor with the boat being tossed and dropped by the waves. The boat was now bouncing side to side and up and down five or six feet making every step difficult. Jay realized it would be almost impossible to pull the anchor up in the existing conditions. It could also take more than an hour, but more likely one or both of them would be tossed overboard during the process.

Jay stepped forward and though only a foot away yelled at the two to get back from the edge and hold the rope. They barely heard him over the howling wind and pouring rain. He then grabbed the rope and with one swift upward slashing motion cut through it with his knife. Immediately the rope disappeared as the anchor plummeted back toward the ocean floor, freeing the boat.

James and Daniel were now totally silent, frozen with fear at what they had just witnessed.

Jay's simple, unbelievable action spoke louder than any shouting or screaming could. Their situation was serious at best, but more likely desperate, and life threatening for Jay to cut his anchor loose.

The two recovered quickly and rushed to the seats amidships where the windshield and partial boat cover gave them a little protection from the fierce wind and bone chilling rain, sleet and occasional hail. Jay made his way to the controls and put the motor in gear.

They all shivered incessantly, soaked to the bone from the freezing rain.   But the rain jackets helped enormously by keeping the cold sleet and howling wind off them, allowing their shivering bodies to begin warming slightly. In spite of their fear a sliver of hope remained alive. The temperature had dropped from a sunny high

47

approaching seventy degrees only an hour or so ago,

to near freezing. The wind chill was now well below

freezing which would have been tolerable had they

been dry.

An hour ago, the three had felt invincible.

They could have conquered the world and any

problem in it. Now, at the mercy of the horrendous

storm and the seemingly feckless ability of the boat,

fear began to possess them as their dire

circumstances started to sink in.

* *

CHAPTER FOURTEEN

Mayday

Jay punched the GPS on to see which direction he needed to go. Visibility was near zero. It was hard to even see the water outside the boat except with every wave some came pouring over the sides. They might as well be blind, unable to find their way by sight. The GPS would show them the way home.

As the GPS lit up, the newest, and possibly biggest problem slowly dawned on them. The satellites' signals couldn't penetrate the thick, water-filled clouds to tell the device where it was or where anything else was.

49

Jay's fear was quickly turning to panic. Never had he been so lost, so desperate. Jay put the motor in gear and pushed the handle forward. The roar of the engine could be heard over the tempest, but the waves tossed the boat up, sideways and back down with little apparent forward movement. All three had to hang on tight to keep from being thrown around or flung overboard.

The waves were eight to ten feet now, tossing the boat like a cork in a washing machine. The boat was taking on more water with the bilge pump no longer keeping up. Thankfully the Thunder Jet was designed to stay afloat even full of water. But with the additional weight of three grown men, and a cooler filled with ice plus at least a dozen forty to sixty pound halibut, it wouldn't be going anywhere fast, even in calm seas.

Jay gripped the steering wheel so tight with one hand that his muscle cramped. His other hand clung to the throttle and his legs were wrapped around the underside of the seat to keep from being ejected.

"Daniel!" Jay yelled forcefully to be certain his words weren't blown away unheard by the howling wind. "Get on the radio and start calling in a Mayday!"

Before Daniel could even move, Jay yelled to James. "James! Get the flares and shoot a couple off."

In a moment, Daniel was on the radio, hollering Mayday into the microphone. James fired one flare, then a minute later another into the storm but lost sight of them within a second in the thick

soup. They were on their own, as alone as they

would be if they were on the far side of the moon.

The chances of anyone seeing their flares or hearing

their Mayday were sickeningly, frighteningly slim.

* *

CHAPTER FIFTEEN

Desperate Thoughts

The three struggled to hang onto the bouncing, floundering boat even though they were totally exhausted from the day's work. Jay battled to keep the bow headed into the waves so the boat wouldn't flip. James determined the direction they needed to go with the compass he found in the small storage area below the bow bulkhead but it was a constant fight to stay on course with the wind and waves. The boat seemed almost like a piece of driftwood afloat in the water.

They were soaked and cold, buffeted by the intense wind and rain, tired and barely able to hang onto the boat, which was slowly filling with water. The three were uncharacteristically silent, filled with fear as the realization of the futility of their situation descended into their weary brains. Their bodies shivered and shook, trying to keep warm, but to little avail.

The motor droned on as the three terrified men silently awaited their seemingly inevitable fate. Different thoughts flooded each mind, thoughts of wives and children desperately loved, promises kept and promises delayed, dreams and hopes unrealized and thoughts of what each wished they could tell their loved ones back home whom they now realized they would never see or hold again barring some miracle.

Thoughts of advice they wished they could impart to their children to help them as they grew up without a father. They yearned for one long,

last, tight hug, one last bedtime story, and one last

precious moment together. They recalled and

replayed their favorite memories with each of their

loved ones in futile, heartrending silence.

* * * * * * * * * * * * * * * * * * *

Content Loons

Three loons floated on the water in tight formation, bouncing contentedly in the swells. They were all but oblivious to the frosty wind whistling past their heads when occasionally, they were momentarily thrust to the top of a wave. Most of their time was spent in the hollow of the wave protected from the chilling wind. Not that it was of any consequence, since a loon's feathers shield it from cold and water better than any clothing ever invented.

The dark, cloud covered sky was puking large cold globs of sleet, which were blown to bits by the wind's furor. Amidst the overall turbulence, the loons were calmly diving for minnows and small fish, enjoying their bountiful feast.

A roaring, unnatural sound penetrated the scene. One hundred feet from the loons' picnic, moved an embattled, struggling, craft. Three terrified fishermen sat inside the boat, tightly clinging to any plastic, wood or metal they could grasp. The faces of the men reflected debilitating panic as their survival pod was tossed helplessly wave crest to wave trough.

* *

CHAPTER SEVENTEEN

Final Battle

The boat rode to the top of a large wave then slid down the side, rolled over, and landed upside down. James clung to the side trying desperately to hang on during the maelstrom, but his head smashed into the metal rail instantly knocking him unconscious. Blood poured from the gash in his head into the freezing abyss.

Jay and Daniel were trapped under the boat but Daniel felt the rail, pulled himself under and to the outside. He pulled the cord on his life vest, which immediately inflated, and propelled him back into the pandemonium above. Daniel's movements were becoming erratic and slow as the cold water was causing his cardiovascular system to shut down from hypothermia.

For a few minutes, he struggled to hold onto the inverted boat hull but then swallowed a mouthful of saltwater when a wave tossed him up and away from the boat. He coughed and choked violently, gagging on the salty water. Daniel's predicament consumed him, allowing nothing else into his mind. He continued to gag, as he gasped for air, panicked that these might be his last desperate breaths.

Just then, Jay who had also freed himself from beneath the boat saw Daniel choking and gagging only a couple yards away. He fought his way over to Daniel and grabbed his arm pulling him slightly higher in the water. The simple act calmed

Daniel, as he realized he was not completely alone in the tempest.

"You okay?" Jay hollered, trying not to let fear show in his voice. "Have you seen James?" he continued although Daniel had not recovered enough to speak. Finally, Daniel's terrified choking diminished as his throat and lungs momentarily cleared.

They yelled back and forth trying to stay together hoping against desperate hope that some miracle would save them. "No, I haven't seen James." coughed Daniel. "He may be the lucky one."

"Do you think anyone heard the Mayday?" Daniel almost pleaded in a shivering, shaking voice.

Daniel was shivering almost uncontrollably now. Six percent body fat provided very little insulation. The cold, blowing sleet pelting their faces felt like rocks hitting them, making conversation difficult. When they turned away from the wind, the pain receded momentarily.

"Do you think there's any chance help is on the way?" Daniel screamed desperately. Jay didn't want to assault Daniel with the truth.

"We can sure hope." He slowly, haltingly yelled back although he felt little hope.

"My kids!" Daniel sobbed. "The baby". His grief was palpable and the weakened condition of his body quashed any optimism. They bounced up and down, for a while on top, then under the water briefly, until their life preservers would float them back to the surface.

The cold water sucked heat from their bodies numbing their feet and hands then arms and legs.

They no longer felt cold or pain. Fear became

horror as the ultimate realization descended upon

two minds.

A powerful wave tossed them into the side of

the boat. They tried to hang on and climb up onto

it, but their fingers, and arms, and legs wouldn't

obey their brains commands. Then as their

coordination and strength diminished they became

quiet, no longer struggling. Eventually the shivering

and shaking ceased.

For several minutes the bodies floated

quietly, giving the illusion that they were at peace in

the cold salty water as they drifted in and out of

consciousness. Within moments their hearts were

silent and the lifeless bodies bobbed with the waves,

kept afloat ironically only by their life preservers.

* *

The three loons were content, well fed by the schools of minnows they had been raiding. It was now nighttime dark, even without the storm, and the loons were exhausted from diving and catching fish. They drifted off to sleep bouncing in the water oblivious to the odd looking things bobbing nearby.

* *

Shanna awoke from a deep sleep to the sound of loud, tormented moaning, and shaking. She cautiously reached out to feel a sweating, shivering form within arm's-length. She pushed hard against it with a frightened cry.

The figure yelled and grabbed for her, wrapping its arms around her. "Oh god, oh god, Shanna? Are you here? Am I here?" The voice paused as if thinking or awaiting an answer. "That was the worst nightmare!" He croaked, panting, still shaking, and realizing he had been dreaming.

Shanna was fully awake now, realizing that Jay was clutching her, squeezing her, terribly upset. He sat up in bed, flipped on a light. His breathing slowed, his quaking began to subside. She sat up next to him as his words began to flow.

"Baby" he was almost sobbing, "Do you remember our near tragedy last night? That I had to cut the fish and anchor loose when the storm assaulted us with huge waves and freezing rain." He paused collecting his thoughts. "You told us that you girls called the Coast Guard when you were at the mall after you checked the progress and intensity of the cold front. You alerted them that we were out there fishing at our favorite spot in my 21' boat and were worried that we might be in trouble based on the speed of the storm and size of the waves."

"Not long after we shot off the flares and called the Mayday, we started heading in." he choked, remembering the futility and desperation they felt at that moment before the rescue. He

composed himself, continuing, "And the Coast

Guard with their big Cutter found us and took James

and Daniel onboard.   They saw our flares only

because they were already close by. If you hadn't

alerted them to our location and situation, they

would never have found us in time and we wouldn't

be here."

He paused and shivered, remembering his

nightmare. "I stayed alone on my boat for an hour

to help steer while they towed it in and got us back

to shore. During the entire hour bouncing in the

boat and hanging on for dear life all I could think

about was how we almost died out there, the

mistakes I made, and never seeing you or Jaece ever

again."

He paused again then continued, "I just had the most realistic, worst nightmare of my life! I dreamt we all drowned. I watched and felt it happen. I was sure I would never see you again. Everything was in such detail. Before you woke me up, I thought I was dead!" They hugged for a long time.

Then Jay shocked Shanna with, "In a couple of days, as soon as the storm clears, I'm going to get the boys and take some bait out in the boat and feed a bunch of loons. And I'm never, ever gonna mess with them again."

* *

The end